MIRACLE IN A SHOE BOX

A Christmas Gift of Wonder

Franklin Graham

with Estelle Condra

ILLUSTRATED BY DILLEEN MARSH

OLIVER
NELSON

THOMAS NELSON PUBLISHERS
Nashville • Atlanta • London • Vancouver

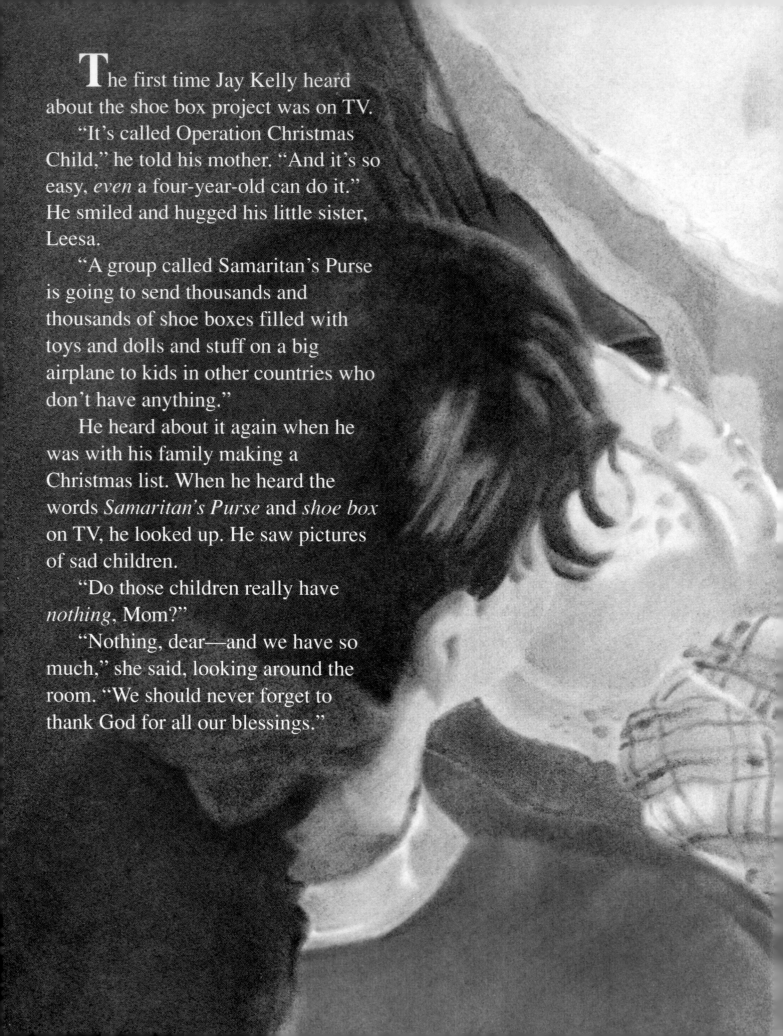

The first time Jay Kelly heard about the shoe box project was on TV.

"It's called Operation Christmas Child," he told his mother. "And it's so easy, *even* a four-year-old can do it." He smiled and hugged his little sister, Leesa.

"A group called Samaritan's Purse is going to send thousands and thousands of shoe boxes filled with toys and dolls and stuff on a big airplane to kids in other countries who don't have anything."

He heard about it again when he was with his family making a Christmas list. When he heard the words *Samaritan's Purse* and *shoe box* on TV, he looked up. He saw pictures of sad children.

"Do those children really have *nothing*, Mom?"

"Nothing, dear—and we have so much," she said, looking around the room. "We should never forget to thank God for all our blessings."

Jay ran to his bedroom. He closed the door slowly and looked around. He couldn't imagine what it was like to have nothing and to be dying from cold and hunger. Then he ran over to his dresser. He pulled out an envelope. On it he had written "Christmas Money."

Jay counted the money three times. Altogether he had 10 quarters, 21 dimes, 6 nickels, and 4 pennies. *That must be enough to buy gifts to fill a shoe box*, he thought.

On Saturday, Jay went with his mom and sister to the store.

Jay fingered his savings as he wandered down the aisles. At the scarves and hats he thought, *I'll give them warm things*. He remembered the newscasts of Bosnia and the children shivering in the snow.

He pulled a red wool hat and blue scarf from the shelf. He took them to the checkout where Mrs. Parker, his Sunday school teacher, was working.

"**W**ell hello, Jay!" said Mrs. Parker.

"I'm buying these to send to Bosnia."

"Bosnia? Sounds important," said Mrs. Parker.

"I'm working on a project called Operation Christmas Child. I'm filling up a shoe box to send to a boy who won't get any presents this year."

"That sounds like something our Sunday school class could do," she said. "Would you tell the rest of the class about it?"

"Sure," he said, as Mrs. Parker rang up the bill. It was more than his savings. Sadly, he took the hat and scarf back to the display.

Then he chose a bar of soap, a tube of toothpaste, a toothbrush, and a tiny toy car. He found a box of crayons and a coloring book on sale.

When Jay was finished, Mrs. Parker put two packs of gum into the paper bag.

She smiled. "These are on me."

"Look," Jay said quietly as he held out his box. "I wanted to give my friend from Bosnia something warm to wear, but I didn't have enough money."

His mom and dad looked up.

"It's okay, Jay," Leesa piped up. "I have some money—I'll help, too."

"Tell you what, let's all help," said his dad, "then we *can* send something warm."

The next day they all went

shopping. With the extra money, Jay was able to get the hat and scarf he'd wanted to buy. Leesa looked at every doll before picking out one with a pink dress, her favorite color.

Mrs. Kelly chose a blanket, some little socks, and a rattle to make a shoe box for a baby.

Mr. Kelly bought a flashlight. "I read that children in war zones are often afraid of the dark," he said. "Maybe this will help."

Jay wrote a letter to his unknown friend: "I am praying for you. I hope you have a Merry Christmas. Love, Jay Kelly." He placed it in the box with his school picture. Then he set aside a five-dollar bill to give to Samaritan's Purse to help pay for sending his shoe box to Bosnia.

"Dad, you know what I would want for Christmas if I were living in Bosnia?" asked Jay.

"What's that, son?"

"For the fighting to stop."

"You know, Jay, we can't stop the war with a shoe box. But we can pray that through the Christmas storybook that Samaritan's Purse is giving to each child, they will find *real* peace—through Jesus Christ."

"Dad, could we pray for my shoe box friend?"

"Sure," said Mr. Kelly, as they bowed their heads.

On Sunday morning, Jay marched proudly into his Sunday school class with the wrapped shoe box under his arm.

As he talked about Operation Christmas Child, his enthusiasm caught on. When Jay finished, all the children decided to join him in making shoe boxes. The pastor even held up Jay's box during the service and asked everyone to take part in the project.

Word spread quickly throughout the whole town. Soon, lots of people were busy filling shoe boxes.

When the Kellys went to church the next Sunday for the special shoe box dedication, Jay was surprised to see boxes piled high in the sanctuary and hundreds more stacked in the fellowship hall.

The pastor had a special prayer asking God to give joy and cheer to the little ones who would receive the shoe boxes. And the pastor prayed for something even more important, that the children would come to know Jesus and the true meaning of Christmas.

The next day, all of the hundreds of shoe boxes were loaded on a truck and taken to the airport. There the shoe boxes from the Kellys' church joined thousands of other shoe boxes already being loaded onto the big cargo plane. Samaritan's Purse would make sure the shoe boxes got to Bosnia by Christmas.

Far away in Bosnia, the war raged on.

Ever since his father had been taken away as a prisoner of war, Adnan Vacek had been helping take care of his mother and Nina, his three-year-old sister. Though he was only nine years old, Adnan had learned quickly how to survive in the war-torn streets of Bosnia.

Their house was destroyed in the fighting, and Adnan found a shelter for them in the cellar of a bombed-out building.

After dark, when the streets were deserted, he would creep out to search for food.

Often the fighting would go on and on. Day and night, they could hear machine-gun fire and bombing. Then Adnan would not dare go out.

Every day they hoped to hear that their father was alive. But there was no news—only the sounds of war and children crying.

Adnan tried to sleep, but was restless.

His empty stomach seemed to roar as loud as the noise outside. His bed—two chairs pushed against the wall—felt harder than usual. After tossing and turning for almost an hour, he finally got comfortable.

He looked over at Nina. Even in her sleep, she looked worried. He thought of his father. His heart sank. Who would take care of them? What would they eat? How long could they survive?

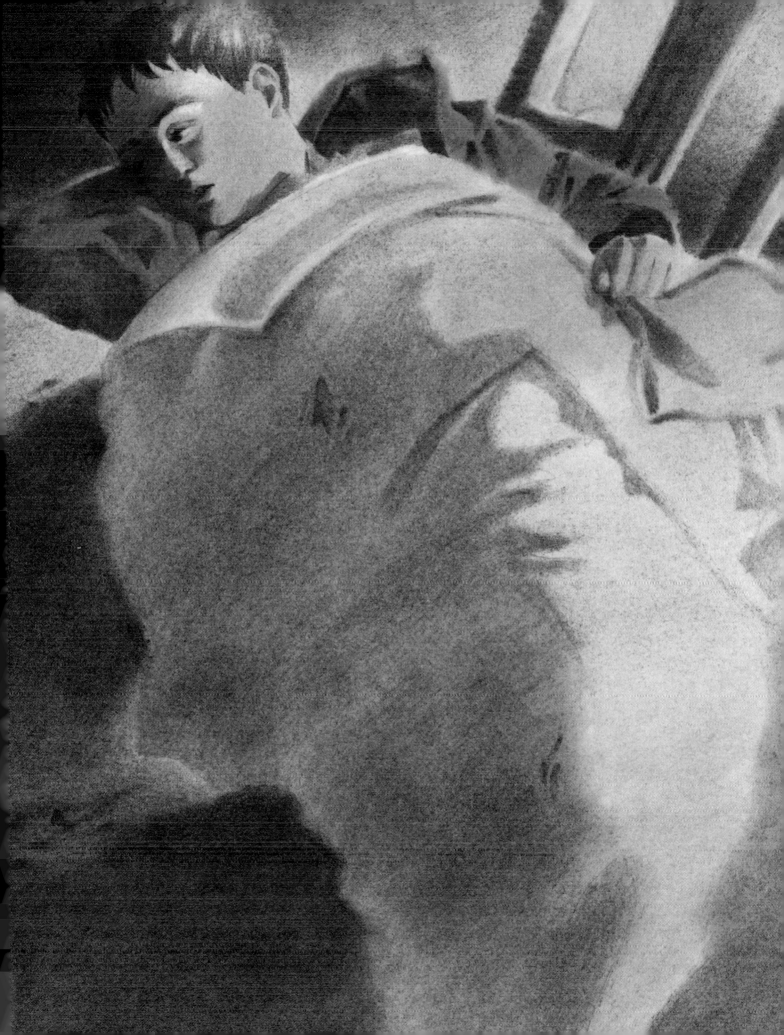

When he stepped onto the street the next morning, he felt the excitement in the air.

"Cease-fire! Cease-fire! Tomorrow is *Christmas*," someone said.

Christmas! Adnan thought. *I forgot all about it. Our house has been bombed and our father has been taken prisoner. What do we have to celebrate?*

"There has been an agreement to stop the fighting," a friend told him. "We must tell everyone to go to the square tomorrow. They're going to exchange prisoners, and a convoy will bring food. There will even be presents for us—from an international Christian organization called Samaritan's Purse!"

Adnan hurried through the dangerous streets to his cellar. He felt hopeful for the first time in months.

The next day, people came out of their hiding places.

A convoy of white Samaritan's Purse trucks rolled slowly down the bombed-out street. When Adnan and Nina arrived with their mother, the trucks were surrounded by men, women, and children. Everyone was eager to catch a glimpse of the precious cargo.

A hot meal, thought Mrs. Vacek, as she watched one of the Samaritan's Purse workers hand a food parcel to her neighbor.

Then a man handed Adnan and his sister boxes wrapped in brightly colored paper.

A doll, hoped Nina. She had dropped hers in the street last year as they ran from a sniper's bullets.

"Merry Christmas," said the man.

Suddenly, there was a far-off roar. Everyone froze.

From across the square, buses appeared.

"The prisoners!" shouted Adnan. Mrs. Vacek clung to her children. The door to the first bus opened, and out stepped a man in ragged clothes. His face was dirty. He had a beard. He was very thin. One by one, the prisoners filed off the bus. Many were wounded. Some had only one arm or walked with crutches.

Adnan's eyes began to fill with tears.

Where is Papa? he thought.

Adnan looked back at the last bus. There were just a few more prisoners left. Through his tears, he saw a tall, thin figure shuffle down the steps. Could it be? But the man looked so old. It couldn't be…

Then their eyes met.

"Adnan! Nina!" cried the man.

"Papa! Oh, Papa!" shouted the children as they pushed through the crowd and jumped into his arms.

Papa had come home.

The family, reunited after many months, made their way back to the bombed-out cellar they called home. Nina and Adnan had been so excited about seeing Papa, they hadn't even opened their boxes.

The Vaceks gathered around the small table in their cellar room. Mrs. Vacek lit a candle. "Open your presents, children," said their father. Mr. Vacek looked at Mrs. Vacek, then at the faces of his little ones.

He thought back to the prayer he had said late one night in prison. "God, if You're out there, show me You care." They were together again. There was food, real food. There were even presents for his children.

"**P**apa!" cried Nina. "A doll! A doll! And she's wearing my favorite color!"

"Look!" said Adnan, holding up a red hat and blue scarf. He pulled the hat over his ears, then he carefully wrapped the scarf around his neck. "They fit just right!" He decided he would wear them always.

Mr. Vacek spotted a children's storybook lying on the table among the gifts scattered there. On the cover was a picture of a young woman and a baby lying in a bed of straw. He picked up the book and began to read the words written in his own language. Everyone watched him curiously. When he finally looked up, his eyes were filled with tears.

"Anya, children," he said quietly, "you must hear this." He opened the book and read each word aloud.

"Our friends in America have shown us they care by sending these wonderful gifts," he said. "But God has given the greatest gift of all—His Son.

"Two thousand years ago, God sent His only Son, Jesus Christ, to die on a cross and save us from our sins. And now, we can ask Him to come into our hearts and forgive us. This Jesus can give us new life. Tonight we will put our faith in Him." Their father bowed his head. One by one, Mrs. Vacek, Adnan, and Nina bowed their heads, too.

When they finished praying, the cellar was still damp and cold. But now, the miracle of God's love warmed each heart.

Dear Jay

My name is Adnan. I am nine years old. My sister Nina is three. There is a war here, and bombs are falling down every day. Our house was destroyed. Our father was in prison, but he is home now.

We got your presents. Everything is so wonderful. Thank you. I like the hat and scarf. They keep me very warm. My sister got a doll from your sister. She didn't have a doll and wanted one very much.

But the best thing you gave us is Jesus. When we got your gifts, Papa read the Christmas story and told us about Jesus. Then we prayed and asked Him to come into our hearts! I am very happy. God gave us the greatest gift of all—Jesus Christ! Now we have true peace.

Your friend,

Adnan

For information on how your family can participate, contact
Operation Christmas Child
Samaritan's Purse
P.O. Box 3000
Boone, NC 28607
704-262-1980

Text © 1995 by Franklin Graham   ❖   Illustrations © 1995 by Dilleen Marsh

Operation Christmas Child, the inspiration and subject of this book, is a project of Samaritan's Purse, an international Christian relief and evangelism ministry to victims of war, famine, and disease.

Editor: Lila Empson; Packaging: Lori Quinn, Amy Clark, Belinda Bass; Production: Brenda White, Bret Snow

ISBN 0-7852-7728-5
Printed in the United States of America.

1 2 3 4 5 6 — 00 99 98 97 96 95